THE

CHRISTMAS

TREE

ABDIEL LE ROY

Copyright 2017 Abdiel LeRoy

License Notes

This book is copyright material and must not be copied,
reproduced, transferred, distributed, resold, licensed, or
publicly performed except as permitted in writing by the
author. Any unauthorised distribution or use of this text is
an infringement of the author's rights.

ISBN
9781521038581

Cover illustration by Ignacio Pessolano

Get the Audiobook!

Get Abdiel's unabridged narration of this book FREE with a trial of Audible US or Audible UK, or purchase wherever audiobooks are sold.

Table of Contents

Preface

I dreamt up this story when living on the Upper West Side of Manhattan, New York City, in the 1990s. Of the many culture shocks I experienced after moving there from London, one of the first was the appalling din of garbage trucks waking me at ungodly hours of the morning.

As a result, I moved to an apartment at the back of the building, but another culture shock came just after Christmas when I witnessed the mass eviction of living Christmas trees on to sidewalks, only to be ground up in the hydraulic machinery of those same trucks.

This story results from imagining the journey of one such tree from forest to market to adornment to abandonment—that is, until grace intervenes.

Enjoy!
Abdiel LeRoy

THE
CHRISTMAS
TREE

Chapter One

There once was a tree. And the tree lived in a great wood. And the tree was surrounded by other trees, its brothers and sisters, for they all came from the same seed. Morning and night, they loved to converse about the things they had seen—about the squirrels who had visited them during the day, about the birds who took shelter among them when the wind blew too fiercely, and about the snows that lay thick about their boughs.

Across their vast togetherness, messages were borne on the air and in birdsong. Merry tales wafted on nocturnal breezes, and laughter echoed back. All was told in a language of love.

And how they loved to dance, swaying in unison as the wind blew, celebrating their very existence. Theirs was a life of secret and endless wonder, that knew nothing of towns and cities or roads or men.

These were conifer trees, clad all year in green. They did not know the cycle of life and death endured by their deciduous cousins who shed their leaves in Winter and who, bare and naked, shivered and trembled through the cold season 'till Spring awakened them, and new growth sprang forth from them and around them. Perhaps, if they had known, they might have been better prepared for what was to come.

It had been a still night, the moon above resplendent in her fullest glory. The trees stood in awed silence before her silver reflection in the motionless white sea of snow at their feet, and watched, spellbound, as the long shadows she cast swept across the milk-drenched ocean beneath them.

When the first pink rays of Dawn crept into view, they had no inkling of danger. When the dim greys of night gave way to a warming array of orange, purple, red and yellow, all seemed to be as it had always been. But it was not. For danger was approaching, danger more terrible than anything they could have imagined, danger that would turn their world upside down and destroy all they knew and cherished.

At first, it sounded like a whisper from the distant reaches of the forest. Yet the forest tides today seemed to stir in a different and unfamiliar tone—a tone of unease and disquiet that rustled through their tender fronds. The stir rose to a restless hum, the hum to a chorus, the chorus to a cry. And the cry to a scream. And a shudder swept through them, a shockwave of consuming terror.

Now, all the forest was astir with panic. We

call it panic, or we may call it pain. But the trees knew not what to call the dread emotion now striking deep at their hearts. For their language had never known such things with which we are all too familiar in our world.

But let us talk about our one very special tree. For before this tree was even a seed, Heaven had conceived him and blessed him and loved him, and had chosen him since before the beginning of Time, before forests even existed or even the earth for them to stand in. And we would not even know this tree were Heaven not our guide.

For now, as we look down in our imaginations upon the treetops of the forest, a divine light descends with us amid the thick mass of green branches, and we enter the heart of the tree the Spirit adores.

That broken morning, our tree trembled in nameless woe, not knowing what trouble befell his cousins and brothers and sisters at the far reaches of the wood. How he wished he could flee, to race across the vales and seek refuge among the neighbouring families of woods whose fame had reached our wood. But our tree had no legs. Or if he did, they were not yet freed from his woody mass. He looked up and wished that he could leap high into the air, or fly as the birds which now raced across the sky above him in loud alarm. But our tree had no wings. The squirrels too ran past in terrified haste, some at his feet, some leaping from branch to branch.

One stopped at our tree, one that had been a frequent visitor to his boughs, his eyes full of woe and pity. He motioned as if to speak, one paw raised and trembling, but he was too afraid, and no sound could utter from his quivering mouth. Only did he manage a frenzied clutch of a branch as if to wish our tree a farewell embrace, before fleeing again.

And now, the copse that had sheltered our tree, nurtured him, and rejoiced over him with singing, became his trap, imprisoning him in a sea of desperation. Only wait now, wait with his fellow trees. Wait in dread anticipation. Wait branch-to-branch, frond-to-frond in comfort of one another, bracing for a terrible impact.

The stir in the forest became a din that turned day to night and joy to wailing. The sound of angry roars came through the forest, louder with every terrifying minute. Then came the sound of voices speaking a language incomprehensible to our tree. But what he could understand from them was a spirit of malice, of fury, of greed insatiable and hate unquenchable. These voices merged with the screams of his kin, a screaming chorus, as each angry roar brought a fresh scream of pain through the horror-laden air.

Through his fellows' fronds, our tree could now make out some movement that caused all the noise. Two-legged creatures appeared, shouting one to another with cruel voices, and each carried an angry-throated thing which he applied to the base of every tree in his path.

And with each stooping of each two-legged creature came another angry-throated roar and a cloud of choking fumes, followed by the sickening sound of torn timber as another companion fell.

Now the older trees, weighty and strong and brave, did their best to protect their younger cousins by holding their branches in the way of the destroyers, and drew attention to themselves by slapping the attackers on their heads or backs with a branch, so as to draw the slayers upon themselves instead. And with an angry curse, the creatures would turn from their intended quarry and slay its protector.

But the noble sacrifice was in vain, except in Heaven, where noble deeds are writ for eternity. For those creatures of carnage, those walking vessels of malice, knew no discernment, cared nothing for beauty, and left not one single tree unfelled in their path.

Now you might think that trees have no eyes, and that trees have no hearts, and that trees have no faces. But look closely at the next tree you see. Is it calling to you? What is it trying to say if we only had ears to hear?

So when our tree saw one of the angry creatures approach his dear sister at his side, he screamed in agony and grief.

"I love thee, brother!" she said, her sad eyes looking into his. And as they cut her, she cried out, her eyes closed and shed their tears.

"Oh my beloved sister," said our tree, his heart full of sorrow, and weeping too. Tightly, their fronds wove in parting clasp. And as she fell, and as her blood poured out on the ground, she uttered her dying sigh, "Goodbye, brother!"

"How can a tree bleed?" you may ask. "And how can a tree shed tears?" It is by the pouring of that which we call "sap", that which flows through the veins of a tree. Other men of greater kindness took the tears lent them by the Maple Tree to make a delicious syrup which they pour on pancakes for breakfast. And will not those precious tears grace a divine banquet one day?

Now braced our tree for the cutting stroke that was to befall him. Weak he felt and trembling, and would willingly have collapsed to the ground to appease his tormentors, rather than suffer the shredding of his timbers and the cut that would forever separate him from the earth he had known and loved, and that had supported his whole life.

But now an angry voice called out to the angry two-legged creature that smote our tree's dear sister, and the creature turned away. He was close enough to smell, though—a reeking, acrid odour that invaded the woody pine-scented forest, a ghastly pall of death and carnage and horror.

The creature silenced his angry-throated thing and convened with his fellows, who now sat down upon the remnants of our tree's kin, which we call 'stumps', put a foul-smelling substance in their mouths, rolled it around, and presently ejected it as a wet, dark-brown clod, staining the once pristine snow. Each in turn then stood to leek pungent yellow fluid on to the ground.

They uttered strange sounds, a bit like laughter, for their bodies shook and their mouths opened to reveal the churning clods that mashed and rolled between teeth as stained as the snow they had just despoiled. But the laughter was born in an alien place, not a laughter of joy, but of destruction that would steal from the innocent and lay waste to beauty.

The stench was overpowering, and our tree and the others around him drew back their fronds in recoil and disgust. Some of the trees, seeing that the carnage had stopped, began to whisper and titter and giggle in the expectation that they had been spared.

But our tree sensed that the destruction was not over—something in the faces of these creatures, the insatiable glint in their eyes, the tension in their bodies, the greedy tones of their speech—and he did not rejoice, but trembled, silently calling to the weeping heavens.

Oh weep, dear tree, to hear the angry-throated things roar again into murderous chorus, weep to see your sap poured out on the ground, weep to see your tender timber shredded, weep at the unutterable pain now coursing through your being. And fall, dear tree, as the world rocks sideways, and feel your own weight crashing onto the frozen waste, and feel your tender boughs crush beneath you. Feel your life draining away into the earth. Weep on the cold ground, and see your branches writhe, not in the sweet tremulous joys of yesterday but in the shuddering horrors of today.

Feel your foot being dragged by rough, callused, and brutal hands across the spoiled snow.

See thy belovèd mountains disappear from view. Hear the groans of your companions dragged behind you and before you. Feel the naked coldness of steel pressing against your yielding, supple, pliant, and once playful fronds. And now feel your companions heaped on top of you. And though you are somewhat comforted to feel their softness above you, that you are not alone, yet you gasp in the crush of needles and branches and wood, amid the choking dark fumes that now engulf you all.

And hate your innocent companions for their injury of you, as they hate you. Yet melt in your heart for their suffering as now you suffer.

Long is the journey as you lurch from side to side in the crush, as you compress under the weight of your fellows. Turn your thoughts upon yourself as you hear their anguished cries, and imagine a better place.

As night falls, the commotion goes on with its sickening jolts and swerves, so that by the time day finally comes, in thy great sorrow and distress thou art barely aware of it.

Now are you all offloaded by those angry, callused hands. Now is the crush relieved, and giddily you stand, mustering some relief. Now you and your kin are surrounded by many more two-legged creatures, who look at you, touch you, converse with their fellow creatures about you, and pass rectangular-shaped leaves one to another.

Your pains have subsided, but still you feel the onset of death and decay. You recall an ancient legend about a mighty ancestor who saved his kin from an evil race, and whose seed began your forest. And you hope that it is true.

Such were the thoughts of our tree and his companions as they stood in the market, and one by one were carried off to a fate unknown.

Chapter Two

Two nights had come and gone since our tree was wrested from his home and hauled into the world of men. And as this third day wore on, and many of his companions were removed, our tree felt lonelier than ever. But then he noticed a smaller two-legged creature looking at him, whose face spoke not of the cruelty our tree had come to expect but of kindness and optimism, innocence and faith. And for the first time since his cruel cutting, our tree began to feel hope rise in his timbered breast.

"Daddy," said the small creature in a high voice, "I like this one!"

Our tree shivered as a bigger creature approached. But it was not a smiting hand that took hold of him; it was one of gentleness, and it gently bore him away. Looking down, our tree could see that the taller creature's limb was touching the limb of the smaller one, in what seemed a gesture of affection, as the two walked side by side.

Now some of the words we use to describe things in this story may strike you as strange. Why say "limbs," when we know that our tree saw the man and his son walking hand-in-hand? The reason is that we are telling this story from the tree's point of view. And at the start of our tale, he knew only the words of the forest, which had never yet seen men.

Now did our tree let fall some sap in tears of gratitude. For in these two creatures he sensed a breed apart from the first assailants. Upon the shoulder of the shorter one did this tear fall.

"The tree's crying, Dad!" said the smaller one, noticing the drop on his garment.

"Goodness me!" said the older one in a deep voice. "What an imagination you have!" And our tree perceived the limb of the taller creature squeeze the limb of the shorter one, as they proceeded.

It was not long before they came to a tall structure, standing against the sky. Through an opening in the side of this structure they entered. Up a hill made of notches they climbed, until they reached an area with straight lines. Confined it was, compared to the great wood, but after his ordeal, our tree was happy to be here.

Set down in one corner of the area and placed upon a vessel containing water, our tree surveyed his surroundings and drank great quaffs that replenished his sap. All seemed bedecked with bright and beckoning objects that sparkled and gleamed in the light.

And many pleasing things were set before our tree. Stretching towards him were a row of red objects that seemed like the garments the two-legged creatures wore on their feet, and each one bulged as if fit to burst with its contents. And in the opposite corner from our tree stood a small furry creature, like a miniature bear, and though motionless, its bright, beady eyes seemed to glint and beckon in eager anticipation of some forthcoming event.

And alongside that bear was a large object with a row of white teeth, with smaller black teeth between them. Our tree was to find out it could make beautiful music when its teeth were pressed down.

And on the top of that object was a collection of miniature two-legged creatures, frozen in gesture and expression. Each appeared to gaze in adoration upon a central creature, smaller and more vulnerable than the rest and lying horizontally in a wooden hollow.

These were all creatures of a kinder, gentler disposition than those who had cut our tree in the forest. And alongside the frozen creatures stood a four-legged beast, also in frozen miniature, and it reminded him of home, where other four-footed creatures frequently traversed the forest floor beneath him.

"I am alive after all," he said to himself, "and kinder creatures now surround me, who mean me no harm."

And indeed, his hopes were realized. For now both two-legged creatures, along with two others who seemed to live there too, set to work around our tree, adorning him with all manner of shiny and glittering decoration, and of such vibrant and varied hue, that they reminded our tree of the rainbows that on occasion would soar in graceful arch over him and his forest kin. And beneath the lower branches of our tree, they placed all manner of brightly wrapped packages that seemed to be filled with love.

Then, as if to crown their design, the tallest creature lifted up the younger one who had first noticed our tree, so that he could place on its top a glorious star that sparkled in the light.

Our tree looked down proudly upon his graceful limbs and thought he was quite a handsome tree and even wished his fellows could see him now. And all the while, the wound of his cut began to heal in the vessel of water at his foot.

Finally, the little boy and his father (for our tree had now learned the difference between a boy and a man and knew the boy to be the son of the man) wrapped a line of shiny ornaments around our tree. And when they connected this line to what they called a "wall," the ornaments lit up in many-coloured brilliance, and this brilliance filled the room as night fell. The tree's heart swelled within his timbered breast in delight. And he played in his fancies with the shadows around and beneath and above him.

He also realized that the young boy had a mother and a sister. And he remembered with sorrow his own dear sister, wishing that she might stand in a room as beautiful as this, and be surrounded by creatures as kind.

Over the coming days, more packages accumulated at the foot of our tree, and delicious fragrances filled the air, and the creatures drank of inspiriting waters and ate good things. They celebrated and danced on their two legs and made music upon that toothed object, which they called a "piano," and sang and told stories and recited poems.

Our tree felt approach a day of great anticipation. This day, he learned, was called "Christmas", and it celebrated the story of another boy who appeared in a winter of a former age — perhaps the age of the ancient forest, our tree thought to himself—and that this was the same boy adored in the depiction of miniatures on the piano.

One of our tree's favourite poems, among the several he heard, was about a certain "Saint Nick". It was splendid verse, he thought, playful and joyous. And he wished he could share it with his fellows from the forest, where poets and poetry were held in the greatest reverence. For poetry was the forest's first language.

Chapter Three

Finally, the day they called "Christmas" seemed imminent. And on the night before, which they called "Christmas Eve," the boy and his sister sat contemplating the wondrous array of colour before them and eyeing the packages beneath the tree and wondering what might be in them.

Suddenly, though, the boy's face saddened. "I wish it could be Christmas all year round," he said.

"Then we could get presents every day," replied his sister.

"And we would always have this beautiful tree to remind us of it," said the boy. "I think the tree wants to stay here forever too."

"Don't be silly," said his sister. "How can a tree *want* anything?"

The question hung unanswered in the fixed gaze of the boy, who saw into the heart of our belovèd tree. And he felt loved *by* the tree. And indeed he was. It was as if they had come from the same origin and would return to the same place.

The children went to bed, and our tree fancied they must be thinking about "sugarplums", whatever they may be. He pondered what he had heard. If Christmas was not all year round, what came *after* Christmas? He had heard this family describe him as "The Christmas Tree". What would become of him if it were not Christmas any more? And could the boy's wish of having Christmas every day come true?

As he comforted himself with this last thought, suddenly a man clothed in red appeared before him. His face was adorned with white hair, and on his head he wore a red cap. He appeared to leave more packages at the foot of our tree, then he turned, stroked and kissed one of his branches, and said "God bless thee, Tree of our Tomorrows!" Then, with a wink of affection, he disappeared again, after which our tree thought he heard the pattering of light footsteps rushing away above him.

He had just returned to quiet contemplation of the bright hues cast by the lights adorning him, when he noticed a stirring among the hitherto frozen creatures on the piano top. The little child around whom the others figures were gathered, appeared to move. His radiance illuminated everyone and everything around him, then filled the entire room in which our tree dwelt, becoming even brighter than the Christmas lights.

Our tree looked about him (for a tree can see in every direction at once), and to his amazement now found himself standing among all those little figures. He knew not whether he had shrunk to their size or whether they had grown to his. But there he was among them, and everyone now seemed to be in motion.

Looking intently upon the child was a young woman, whose tresses lay upon her comely shoulder.

"Blessed art thou among women!"[1] said a voice, like the sound of rushing waters.[2] But the tree could not see who spoke. Alongside her was a tall man. His hands were callused but gentle, strong to defend yet tender to caress, and conjured none of the dread of those bitter hands that first smote our tree in the once enchanted wood.

Kneeling around the child in adoration were six other men. Three held each a staff in his hand, and each placed it at the foot of the child, and three others removed crowns from their heads and placed them alongside the staffs. They were trying to converse with eachother, but the men who had staffs spoke a different language from those who wore crowns. So presently they tried to convey their meaning through gesture.

The men of the crowns pointed upwards. Our tree looked, and saw to his delight the open night sky, thick inlaid with patterns of bright gold,[3] where the stars appeared to be singing, a huge choir in joyful assembly.

And our tree remembered the choirs whose music he had heard in former days, when the younger saplings would sing with high voice, and the older trees, venerable and ancient giants, with low voice, and others with a pitch inbetween.

And now the singing orbs of the night sky appeared to be paying homage to one new star, brighter than all the rest, that blazed with a glory that illuminated all the upturned faces.[4]

The men of the staffs, when they beheld this brightest of all stars, seemed to understand what the men of the crowns were trying to tell them. For they said "Oh!" and "Ah!" (And perhaps "Oh!" and "Ah!" are words that *every* language understands.)

Then the men of the staffs tried to convey something back to the men of the crowns. They too pointed to the sky and got to their feet and flapped their arms. Seeing their message was not understood, the three started singing. Or trying to. But they couldn't seem to agree on a tune. One would hum a note, the other two would try in vain to copy it, and the three would sing for just a few moments before collapsing with laughter.

And all around them laughed too — the baby in the centre, the young woman with the compassionate eyes, the taller man beside her, the men with the crowns, and even the four-legged beast. These antics continued until none could remain on his feet any longer but fell to the ground in convulsions of mirth. And our belovèd tree saw for the first time the appearance of sap at their eyes, but knew that this meant joy, not sorrow.

Finally, as the laughter began to die down, the three men of the crowns started conversing with each other, repeating the antics of the men with staffs, and gradually appeared to understand the message their friends had tried to convey.[5] At once, they stopped talking, looked at eachother, and uttered "Ohhhhhhhh," which set the whole company to screeches of laughter once more. The very pillars of that place seemed to tremble with laughter, and even our tree felt his boughs shaking and his trunk swaying as he caught the spirit of mirth that blessed this place.

But now, amidst the laughter, the baby creature seemed to take the appearance of a full-grown man! And the man said to our tree, "I am that star that appeared to you in the heavens. And I am come to bless thee. I established thee in Eden, thou died'st with me at Calvary, and thou art chosen to celebrate the day of my birth. Thou wilt ever stand with me by the River of Life, and thou shalt bear twelve crops of fruit, and thou shalt heal the nations."[6]

And as our tree heard these words, daylight filtered into his vision, and the laughter belonged to children—not just the boy and his sister but others too—who danced around the room to shouts of "Merry Christmas!" And shrill notes were blown from musical instruments that unrolled themselves. And the children tore into the packages around the foot of our tree and embraced and kissed each other. And the people—for now our tree had learned to call them "people" rather than "creatures"—sang around the musical instrument and laughed some more and teased each other and supped hot drinks and ate choice things.

How glorious it all seemed to our tree, who realized he had had a dream, or something like it. How happy he was to be surrounded by love and laughter and merriment and warmth and rejoicing. Now, a red-coated figure came into the room. He reminded our tree of his dream, though the red of this figure was brighter, and the white on his face more like a cloud. Some of the younger children called him "Father Christmas" and others called him "Uncle". But he too brought more packages, which the children tore into with delight.

But our special tree paid special attention to

the special little boy who had brought him there. And he rejoiced to see the child's eagerness and delight. Presently, in a moment of reflection, the boy turned his attention to the piano and to the collection of figures thereon.

"Daddy!" he exclaimed. "The shepherd's sticks and the wise men's crowns are on the ground now. Do you think they had a party in the manger last night?"

"Bless me!" said the boy's father. "What an imagination you have!"

"I bet you moved them!" said his sister.

"No I didn't," said the boy.

"Let him alone," said their father gently. "Who knows what magic happens when we're not looking."

Our tree tried to speak now, for he so wanted to tell them what he had seen that night. Heaving within himself, he tried to stir his branches as he used to do in the forest when he wanted to speak to his brothers and sisters.

"The Christmas Tree would know if they had a party, wouldn't you?" said the little boy.

And perhaps our tree did manage to wave a frond or two, for the little boy said, "Look, he's nodding!"

"Don't be silly!" said his sister. "It's just a tree!"

But the boy continued to gaze at the branches.

As day drew to a close, guests and loved ones started to drift away, until the room was left with only the immediate family. Quietly, they sat on chairs facing our tree, drinking a brew, and discussing the events of the long day.[7]

"Alright," said the father eventually. "Time for bed."

The little boy lingered as the others departed.

"Good night, Mr. Christmas Tree!" he uttered.

And perhaps the little boy discerned as he left the room, the tremble of a frond, the dipping of a branch, or a twinkle of the star that stood atop our tree.

Chapter Four

And so twelve days and twelve nights passed. Our tree knew this, because he heard the family talk of "Twelfth Night."

"Alright then, time to take down the decorations," said the father, "though it seems a shame."

Gently, he plucked the bright star from the top of our tree and placed it in a container. And the little girl severed the line of bright lights from its source in the wall, and they were suddenly extinguished. The little boy removed but one bright red sphere from the tree and stood staring distractedly at our tree's reflection in its mirrored surface, while the others worked around him. He was in that state of mind where we take great interest in trivial things to distract us from some big thing that causes us sorrow or fear.[8]

And the face of the little boy was so sad that our tree began to feel afraid himself, and watched with alarm as he was steadily stripped of every bauble, every decoration, and every strand.

He felt exposed and vulnerable now, though he knew not what to call this feeling, for in the forest none had ever known or heard of it. He cringed with foreboding as the boy's father, with a look of reluctance, approached our tree and hoisted him on his shoulder again.

The little boy sat silently on a chair, his lower lip curled downward and his face wet with tears, and our tree too, as he was carried back down the notched hill, wept to be wrenched again from his second home of comfort and delight.

But none heard him. Only the boy looked up and thought he saw the branches beckoning to him as our tree was carried away. But, too overcome with sorrow, he buried his face in his hands.

And as our tree was brought outside, he began to understand the horror of what it meant for Christmas to be over, to be loved only for a season and then cast out.

"Goodbye now!" said the boy's father, propping our tree up against another taller tree, whose base was planted in the ground.

Then he turned back and walked inside the structure he had left, and disappeared with a thudding sound that struck the air with doom.

Now was our tree alone, very alone. Never had he felt so alone in all his life. For even in the misery of his cutting and in the terrible journey afterwards, and in that place where men exchanged trees for rectangular-shaped leaves, he had at least been in the company of his forest fellows.

He began to feel cold, a sensation he had never known before. And he knew not whether it was coldness of temperature or the chill in his heart. The ground beneath him was hard and grey, and in the fading light of dusk stretched in a straight line between a row of structures like the one our tree had just left.

Exhausted and frightened, he wept. And his sap poured out onto the hard grey ground.

"Tough break, kid!" said a voice.

Our tree stirred to see who had addressed him.

"Up here!" said the voice.

He looked up to see the face of the tree whose trunk he rested against. It was faded, grey, weary, yet seemed to offer a token of kindness in these bleak surroundings.

"I see youse guys get trown outta dese houses every yee-ah. And I says to myself 'Dat's gotta hoit!' Ya get cut down where ya grow, dey bring you inta dis stinking city, dey dress you up for a few days, den dey trow you outonda street. I was a young sapling like you when dey pulled me outa de ground, but at least I gotta keep my roots, ya know. And at least I got ta stay in one …"

At this he broke off, apparently not wanting to finish his thought.

"Still, you came from a good house," he continued. "Some a dose udder houses, dey got cats an' dahgs, an' ya don't even wanna *know* what dey can duda trees! And some a ya friends get put nexta radiators. And some don't even get no wahdah!"

Our tree pondered these words, but gave no answer.

So the big tree went on, "Ah, so you had ya fifteen minutes of fame, kid, whatya gonna do?"

"How do you know all this?" our tree asked feebly.

Now you may ask, "How can a tree speak?" Well, if you or I stood next to these two trees on that cold winter morning, we would have heard nothing, except perhaps the stirring of twigs and the wind blowing through branches. But they do talk, only not in words that we understand. And we must go to that Spirit who first blew through the ancient forest to interpret for us.

" 'Cos I tawk to youse guys every yee-ah after Christmas," said the taller tree. "And my buddies on the street—ya see dem ovah dere?"

Our tree looked, and saw two parallel lines of trees similar in appearance to the one he leant upon.

"We're beech trees. Da people call dis an

31

avenoo, but dat's to give it class dat don't belong. Anyways, my buddies tell me 'bout da Christmas trees put out by dem. Ya see ya brudders 'n sisters along dah sidewawk?"

Our tree looked again in the dim grey light and saw his fellows from the great wood strewn upon it. Only one or two had been propped up as he.

Anguish shot through his heart at the devastation wrought upon his kin, once the pride of the forest, whose joy had turned to despair, as now he heard their faint whimperings and groans.

But one voice he recognized, and his heart filled with hope, compassion, and longing. For it was his sister, hewn from his side in the great forest, now lying but a short distance from him.

"Sister!" he called.

No answer.

"Sister!" he called again, louder this time.

"Brother?"

She looked from her fallen position on the cold grey ground and saw our tree and inwardly rejoiced. But great was her pain, and our tree knew she was dying a second death, as indeed they all must die. They must die because they were beautiful and did no harm.

"It is I," said our tree. "My heart joys to see

you."

"Brother, what will become of us?"

"I do not know. All I know is that they love us only at Christmas, for they call us "Christmas trees", and that Christmas comes but once a year, and when it is over, they have no use for us any more."

"That is what I thought," said his sister. "Then we are doomed to perish."

Our belovèd tree thought for a moment, aching to comfort her.

"But the one who brings Christmas, the one whom Christmas celebrates, the child creature who became a man, promised me that I would always stand with him by the River of Life, and he said I would heal the nations."

"I pray you are right," said his sister, "but how do you know all this?"

So our special tree recounted his dream — about the figures who came to life, about the belovèd child and its parents, about the three men with the staffs and the three men with the crowns, about the bright star in the sky, and about the man who had brought him this message.

Amazement fell on his two hearers, and our tree felt he had brought a message of comfort to them both.

"Then we have hope, even if we should die a second death," said the tree's sister. At this, weak with sorrow, she fell asleep.

"Whoa kid, I guess ya got d'anointing or somet'n," said the beech tree. "I hoyd about a place where nutt'n dies and dere's no more grief or loss.[9] But I neva believed in such a ding. But if this Christmas guy's fa real, he's ow-ah ticket to a bedda place!"

Night fell. And our tree watched with disgust as large rodents appeared, and crawled over the cold grey ground and over the trunks of his prostrate friends. These were not the gentle, inquisitive animals that hopped, sprang, or clambered through the forest—rabbits, squirrels, badgers, and the like—but dirty, thieving, and voracious vermin, that fed on refuse and garbage. And our tree shuddered at the sight of them.

And they had scarce disappeared and the dawn had scarce begun to assert her weary and unwilling presence on the bleak grey city, when our tree was stung from his fitful sleep by a thunderous roar that reminded him of the angry-throated things he heard that terrible day when he and his kin were rent from their forest home.

But this engine made a deeper noise, yet more horrible, yet more menacing and relentless, that made the very earth tremble. Our tree saw two glaring lights pierce the gloomy scene. And on it came—a terrible, huge, angry white monster that roared and screeched, and spawned angry creatures that jumped down and pulled the discarded Christmas trees from the cold, grey ground, and fed them into the back of that angry, white, relentless monster.

And though our tree could not see behind this white rolling giant, it appeared to be consuming his kin. For they screamed and cried out in their final death throes. Some of the trees in the path of the monster prayed for life, but many prayed for death and for a swift end to their suffering. And one by one, each was picked up and thrown thoughtlessly into the devouring white monster.

Again our tree trembled, and thought of the one who had promised him eternal life, and cursed him for his absence now in the hour of need. And our tree wished he had never existed, had never known beauty, friends or brothers or sisters, songs or choirs or stars, that he had never even known that he could exist.

He looked up to the beech tree he was leaning against. He had lived there all these years, had seen everything; surely he would know escape from this onslaught. But that tree was asleep now, oblivious to the din, having slept through such chaos many times before. Besides, he was a deciduous tree, who shed all his leaves in winter, and there was not much else for him to do in this dark season but to sleep and wait.

"Help!" our tree cried out, but the beech tree kept on sleeping. "Help!" he cried again, but the monster kept approaching. "Help!" he screamed with every fiber of his being, but his fellow trees kept falling victim to the ravenous, grinding, consuming jaws of the great white beast that plied its monstrous trade.

Chapter Five

The boy spent a restless night, his dreams full of fear and flight, darkness and destruction. One moment he was enjoying a peaceful picnic with his family, the next they were all being swallowed up in an earthquake, a great forest falling in on top of them. He woke with a start, and realized the thunder and rumble he had heard in his dream was a garbage truck coming down the street.

Running to the window, he looked down at the scene of devastation below. The men were about their business with all haste, and none thought and none felt and none reasoned and none listened. But the little boy looked at his tree propped up against the beech tree, saw the terrible jaws devouring every other tree on the street, and felt panic in his heart.

Running downstairs, he reached the cold grey pavement just as the great white monster was drawing alongside his tree, saw the men that swarmed from it, and the hungry jaws churning the mangled limbs of other trees as the sap bled from their barks. But even worse was the sound of those terrible jaws devouring, chewing, grinding, roaring as if to cry, "More! More! More! More!"

Of course, the boy knew he was watching a

garbage truck going about its customary business; it was a familiar sight on this street. But as he witnessed its carnage, destruction, and indifference to life, his heart became that of a terrified tree, and he raced towards the scene as fast as his legs could carry him, his bare feet slapping the cold grey ground.

Now, one of the men seized on the tree that lay nearby our little boy's tree.

"Dear brother," said our weeping sister, "they have come to take me away now. We go to a second death. But my heart is revived by your story."

"I will follow thee and meet thee in a better place," our tree replied.

"By the River of Life," said his sister.

"By the River of Life," answered our tree, choked with tears that dropped onto the cold grey ground, as honey on ice.

Our tree saw and shuddered in horror as one of that heartless crew seized his sister and hauled her towards the mechanical monster. And as he dragged his quarry along, a second man came the other way.

Speed surged into the boy's legs as he raced towards our tree, his heart pounding. The man reached, the boy ran, the man grasped, the boy ran, the man lifted the tree, the boy arrived.

"No, please don't kill him!"

"What's ya problem?" said the man.

The boy looked up in fear. He barely reached the man's waist.

"What's ya problem?" the man barked again.

"Please sir, don't put the tree in the garbage truck!"

"Now look, I gotta job to do. This tree goes in the back just like the rest of 'em!"

The scene was beginning to attract the attention of the other men, who paused from their work to walk over.

"What's up?" said one.

"This kid's telling me not to kill the tree!" he shouted back.

At this, the men burst into laughter. Our tree shuddered, remembering the horrid laugh of that first gang who had torn him from the forest.

By now, the monster had ceased to rumble, and the driver stepped out.

"What's goin' on?"

"This kid's telling me not to kill his tree!" said the first man.

Again, the others roared with laughter.

"The one wearing the pyjamas!" said another.

And the crew laughed some more.

By now, the beech tree woke up. For this event was unusual enough even for him to notice.

"Hey kid, what's up?" he said.

"The little boy's trying to save me," said our tree.

"I tell ya, kid. Dere's an angel looking out fa you!"

"But they took away my sister."

"I know, kid. She got an angel too but … just in a different way."

Now, faces were starting to appear through the transparent holes of the adjacent dwellings. One of them was that of the boy's father.

"What are you doing out there, Son?" he said. "Barefoot? And in your pyjamas?! You'll catch your death!"

"I'm trying to save the tree!" the boy replied.

"Wait there!" said his father, and disappeared inside again.

Meanwhile, the driver of the white roaring monster was becoming increasingly agitated.

"We don't got time for this! Put the tree in the back of the truck. Move it!"

"Sorry kid. I got my job to do," said the one holding our tree. And he started walking away.

"No!" said the little boy, running after, and holding his tree with all his might.

The man stopped and turned. He was much bigger than the boy and certainly could have overpowered him. But something in his nature made him stop, for he had not lost that spark of divine instinct that wants to protect, rather than injure, someone or something who is vulnerable and defenceless.

And perhaps such an instinct guided the other men, who tried to prise the tree out of the boy's hands without harming him.

But the boy refused to let go, and his naked feet braced against the cold grey concrete, and his face scalded with tears, and his heart beat fast from running and fear, and his arms clutched his belovèd tree for all he was worth. And I think he must have been worth rather a lot, this little boy. For though he held on with the arms of a child, he was compelled by the heart of Heaven.

And trumpets were now heard in that Heaven by those with ears to hear, and the stars above, observing unobserved, sang their triumphant "hallelujahs", and the Holy Countenance wept with joy, and the angels fashioned a splendid crown of gold and diamonds for the boy to wear, and a sword made of Heaven's steel and tempered in the furnaces of Hell, for the boy to wield when he grew to manhood.

And the soul of the ancient forest now swayed in the wind and whispered through its fronds and clapped its hands, and the Spirit that led us in sharing this story saw the soul of the boy in his white-hot magnificence. And all rejoiced, hearing the words: "This is my son, whom I love. In him, I am well pleased."[10]

"Look kid, let the tree go, alright? I gotta job to do," repeated the man holding our tree. But now came the strong arms to uphold the strong heart.

"That's enough now, then!" said the boy's father, who by now had reached the scene. "If he wants the tree, let him have it!"

The men fell to silence. There were several of them, and only one of him. But there was something in the fierceness of his look that spoke of courage and dauntless determination, and he commanded respect in the hearts of that crew.

After all, for them this was just a delay in their schedule, an inconvenience, but to the boy and his father, this was a claim to something so precious that not even the wealth of all the world could purchase it.

"I'll be taking that!" said the boy's father, and hoisted our tree back on to his shoulder for the third time.

"Hey kid!" the weather-beaten beech called

out. "Like I said, you got d'anointing or somet'n!"

Chapter Six

His heart full of gratitude and relief, our tree was borne away from the white monster and its agents of death, who stood amazed as the boy and his father and the tree departed.

Once again, the three of them approached the structure where the boy's father first brought the tree, but instead of going inside this time, they went around the back and reached an area with green ground and patches of snow.

"Thank you for saving the tree, Daddy!" said our little boy.

"Well it was you that did the saving. But if you thought they were going to kill him, we'd best not let him linger on the street," replied his father, "but goodness me, what an imagination you have!"

Putting the tree gently against a wall, he fetched an implement and proceeded to dig a hole in some earth adjacent to the grass. When deep enough, he placed the trunk of our belovèd tree into it. "Well, let's just see how he does here," said the father. "Perhaps he'll get another chance of life!"

He replaced the earth while the boy held onto the trunk. And the tree loved the boy and felt his embrace.

"There now!" said the father. "He'll never have to leave this spot as long as it likes him to stay here. And next Christmas, we can decorate him out here and never have to disturb his peace and quiet. Alright now then, that's enough excitement for one day. Let's go in and have ourselves some breakfast!"

And hoisting the boy on his shoulders, off he went inside the structure.

Our tree felt safe. He would not be lonely again with the boy to take care of him. Nor would he be removed again. But how his heart pined for his sister. How he wished she could be planted there right next to him, as in their former days in the forest. And he shed a drop of precious sap.

The boy came out again several times that day to check on his fronded friend, though he could not bear to see how much he had suffered. Our tree looked down and saw that so many of his beautiful needles had fallen off, and that some of the remaining ones had turned brown. And he wept, for he had been accounted a splendid tree in the forest. All the other trees had said so. And in his former days, he had taken much joy in the suppleness of his limbs and in the abundance of his needles and in the admiration he had stirred among the animals and birds of the forest. But now, he was even bereft of those gay Christmas adornings that had cheered him and beautified him only yesterday.

"Good night, Mr. Christmas Tree," uttered the little boy, whereupon he turned slowly and went back inside.

At that moment, our tree was startled by the flapping of wings against his branches, and he saw a bird. Quite an ordinary bird, he thought, drab and brown in colour, not like the exotic varieties he had known in the great wood, not as beautiful, he thought, nor as well groomed.

"Go away!" thought our tree. He did not want to be rustled and bothered now, but to be left in peace to contemplate his dishevelled appearance. And he looked away from the troublesome bird, that flitted its tail and tilted its head this way and that in rapid motion.

"What kind of a welcome do you call this?" said the bird.

"I'm sorry," said our tree. "It's just that I've rather a lot on my mind right now."

"Yes I heard. I got the news from your friend across the way, you know, that tall beech tree? He said you and he had become acquainted. And he asked me to tell you 'Good Luck'. He also told me you're quite a celebrity round these parts. All the trees and birds are talking about you. And they say the boy who rescued you is very brave. Anyway, the beech tree thinks you'll eventually grow tall enough to see over the roof and talk to him directly. But in the meantime, he asked if I would be your messenger. Would you like that?"

"That's most kind of him," answered our special tree. "Please convey to him my deepest gratitude."

"What eloquence!" said the sparrow. "I suppose that's how you all talk out there in the great Wild Wood? The King's Woodlish!" he said with a flourish of his wing and the suggestion of a curtsy.

At this, the sparrow found himself so amusing that he almost fell off the branch with laughter. And even our sorrowful friend managed an inward smile at his new, amusing little companion.

"Anyway, the beech tree says, if you ever get lonely, just send word through me."

"Thank you!" said our special tree.

"Fuggedaboud it!" said the sparrow again, affording himself another merry chuckle. "And if you ever feel low, just look up. That's where the sky is, and the stars, and us birds."

At this, he flitted away. Our tree watched in amusement as his new-found friend darted and

47

weaved around the garden until he focused his acrobatics on a flying insect and pursued it over the top of the structure — which our tree now knew to be called a "roof" — and out of sight.

Chapter Seven

Our tree now stared at the darkening sky. The first few stars were beginning to appear. Not as brightly as he remembered from his forest days, but they were, as the sparrow had suggested, a great comfort to see, especially when our tree felt so discouraged at looking down at himself.

How long he stared at the sky, we cannot tell. But it had turned to black and the stars were peeping out, when he noticed one star brighter than the rest, that blazed triumphantly and gloriously, and seemed to be a sign of hope. Brighter it grew, and brighter still, coming closer now, until it flooded our tree and his surroundings with a radiance that poured into every nook and drove away every shadow. And it reminded our tree of that brightest star he had seen in his dream, when the three men with the staffs and the three men with the crowns adored the infant boy.

The light was so dazzling that our tree was momentarily blinded. But when he could see again, he found himself in a sun-drenched glade at midday, surrounded by other trees of every type, many laden with blossoms and even fruit. Never had he seen such trees before. How beautiful they were! A cooling wind made their leaves quiver, casting playful shadows on the ground, and their resplendent flowers in many shades of colour swayed and cast their fragrance on the air.

Ahead was a waterfall of crystal light that fed a sparkling stream. And lo, by that stream stood a vision of feminine loveliness. Her serene presence seemed all joy, all peace, and her flowing robes were of sheer white. Our tree thought her the loveliest creature he had ever seen, neither tree nor human, something akin to both perhaps, only lovelier by far than any he had ever seen. Gilded was she in Heaven's own light. A goddess perhaps, or a nymph. For our tree had heard legends of such creatures who had once roamed the earth. Dazzled by this vision, he was dumbstruck as she spoke.

"Dear brother!" she called.

Could it be her, the one he had called "Sister", his dear companion of the forest, his forlorn neighbour on the cold grey ground, now transformed into this vision of transcendent loveliness?

"Come!" she called to him, and held out her arms—for arms they were, and draped with a shimmering white fabric.

And though he wondered *how* he could move to her, instinctively he stepped forward, for now he had two legs, as we do. He expected his steps to be heavy and clumsy and awkward. But to his surprise, they were light and nimble and easy.

Into his sisters arms he ran, and they wept together, wept from eyes. For now they had eyes that we would recognize.

I can not tell you how long they embraced, for where they were, there is no such thing as time. Nor is there death or sickness, mortality or destruction, but everlasting life.

Our tree stepped back.

"You are so very beautiful!" he said.

"And how handsome you are!" she replied.

She took him by the hand and led him upstream along the brook until they reached a pool of clear, cool water.

"Look!" she said, pointing down.

He did, and gasped to see the handsome face looking back at him, his tall, muscular frame, nor tree nor human, but more splendid than either, god-like in appearance, angelic. He reached a now dexterous hand to the water's surface. And lo, how the surface rippled and gleamed and sparkled!

"Where are we?" he asked.

"We are in the place where nothing dies, and there's no more grief or loss. We are in that place you told me of. The stream by which we stand flows into the River of Life. Here is Paradise, where the Divine Presence looks with favour upon us."

"Then I shall stay here forever with you."

His sister looked down.

"Yes, my brother, but not yet. You must first return to the little boy and his father, for you shall gladden their hearts."

Our tree felt sad. For no matter how comforted he was in the little garden behind the structure in which the little boy lived, he yearned to stay here in this place called "Paradise", to enjoy its glades, its waterfalls, and to be here forever with his sister.

"But come, let me show you this world!" she said, taking him by the hand again.

"Run, Brother, run!" she urged.

And run they did, and with what speed — faster, it seemed, even than the swiftest birds he had seen in the forest. Now his sister let go of his hand, and they ran side by side, faster and faster, but never tiring. Her long graceful limbs swept over the ground in vast strides. She was as swift as she was beautiful, like an arrow's flight. But our tree had no trouble keeping up with her. They ran through fields full of harvest wheat[11] and leapt over rivers and glades and down into valleys and up over hills, and never tired.

And now they approached the base of an

enormous mountain, whose snow-covered peak loomed higher than any he had ever seen. It dominated the horizon like a mighty fortress, and seemed to touch the top of the universe.

Our tree looked at his sister, wondering how they would ever ascend its steep, slippery sides. Seeing his consternation, she chuckled and took his hand. And took him up. And up and up and up they soared. Our tree let out a cry of glee, for he was now flying, flying without wings, and the side of the mountain seemed to race downward as they ascended. Higher and higher and higher they flew, until they even surpassed the peak. And continued ascending.

Beneath them now was a great alpine vista with innumerable peaks. Beyond it, they could see the rivers of this great otherworld, and its oceans and cities too. But these cities were not the cold grey edifice of decay he saw after he was hewn from the forest. They had streets of gold, buildings of sapphire, walls sparkling with jewels, gates of pearl.

"Fly, Brother, fly!" said our sister. And she let go of his hand again. And he flew unassisted, he knew not how. He flew simply by wishing to fly, changed direction merely by wishing to, and his speed was faster or slower as he desired.

Now our sister pointed to a great forest adorning a mountainside, like the one they had grown up in, with its tall trees swaying in the wind. And as our siblings descended to look more closely, they saw that the trees had faces, and that the faces were smiling, and now they had hands, and the hands were waving, and now they had voices, and the voices were cheering; now they had legs, and the legs were running, and now they had wings, and the wings were flying.

Our nymph siblings were joined in the air by a vast multitude of their airborne companions, who flew around them and over them and below them and hailed them with greetings. And our tree recognized among them his dear kin from the forest, and hailed them back.

Now, the wingèd nymphs fell behind our wingless pair, and the whole multitude swept across that limitless sky in great triangular formation. From mountain ranges, they proceeded over plains, and from plains to canyons, and from canyons to rivers. Delighted and enthralled, our tree gasped, though not from exertion but from excitement and joy.

"Now, let us have some fun!" said his sister, as if this were not fun enough already, and soared again to a great height. And taking her brother's hand, she flew up and up and over and over and upside down. And looking down from his upside-down position, our brother saw the great skein of his kin streaming below him.

Having traced a great loop in the sky, the host flew vast leagues but in no time at all, and passed over a massive sea that sparkled invitingly. Suddenly, they all dived down, hurtling toward the blue waters. In a moment, they pierced its crystal-like surface and plunged into its light-filtered depths.

Our pair kicked their feet, for their bodies were supple and lithe, not bound by the stiffness of bark, and reaching great speeds, they leapt from the water like dolphins, plunged again, while their kin leapt and played alongside them, using their wings to fly underwater.

There, they saw yet more wonders, great fish of every colour, that frolicked among golden corals and jewelled rocks and called to them, and great leviathans of the sea who winked their little eyes or waved their fins in greeting.

Now approaching the opposite shore of that vast sea, they surged joyfully through the rolling waves then leapt up into the air again.

And up they flew, up and up and up, as the sky became increasingly colourful, with swirls of orange and pink and rose and purple, then traces of green and blue. Onward and upward, onward and upward until, emerging in the distance to his right, our tree espied another multitude of creatures on a parallel course. Like a delicate pink ribbon was their appearance as they fluttered through the sky on bright wings, followed by a trail of sparkling silver. Breathtaking in beauty, they stirred in the heart of our tree great love.

Not long had he gazed at them when his sister pointed out another multitude on their left, a band of mighty wingèd warriors, clad in bronze breastplates and wearing helmets with great white plumes streaming behind them. Some carried spears and shields; others were more lightly armed with a bow and quiver of arrows. Some had beards on their heavy, square jaws; some were youthful in appearance with curly locks framing their chiselled features. But all were splendid, powerful and mighty, courageous and valiant in appearance.

Yet, splendid as these two great hosts were, they seemed no less enthralled by the appearance and glory of our nymphs. One of the warriors nodded to *our* nymph, which made him feel very special, and he returned the gracious gesture learned from his forest days, when older trees taught the younger ones how to bow with reverence. And our tree fancied that this warrior resembled the father of the little boy and must be of the same tribe.

Soon, our multitude was surrounded by all manner of other multitudes on all sides, flying in formation, including dragons, great wingèd unicorns, and all manner of mythical creature.

Then suddenly, the sky filled with a great rushing and roaring sound, and lit up with golden radiance. Spellbound, our nymph saw arriving on each flank of the multitude of multitudes, a great host of divine beings clad in white and gold, with faces that shone in brilliance almost too bright to behold. "The angels!" our sister whispered to him.

Now, our tree began to doubt his place. "Who am I," he thought, "to be among such company, such great creatures, let alone in the vanguard? What am I doing here?"

He felt himself begin to weaken, started to feel faint, to lose altitude, and feared he would fall headlong on to the horn of a unicorn below.

But one of the great angels, seeming to sense our nymph's unease, surged ahead of his own multitude with a sudden burst of mighty wings. Turning, he approached with his hand stretched forth. He was holding an object that itself clasped something hot and glowing with fire.

Now there is nothing a tree fears more than fire. Even cutting by men with angry-throated machines is not as terrible. So our nymph suddenly convulsed with terror and disbelief. In a flash, he imagined that this vision had all been a cruel hoax, a trap to lure him to an extreme, slow, and painful death.

"Be not afraid!" whispered his sister.

At this, a few of our nymph's brethren supportively nestled around our tree.

"It's alright," said another. "You won't be hurt."

Thus, our nymph allowed the bright glowing ball to near him, and to touch him on his lips.[12] With that, warmth surged through his entire being and filled him to overflowing, and he immediately forgot all doubt and fear.

Now, the angel accelerated before the great host, provoking great admiration from all. And our tree became aware that he too was the centre of attention. Some of the female nymphs were blushing.

"Wow, he got Gabriel!" he heard one whisper.

"That's Gabriel!" his sister echoed in awe. "He stands in the presence of God!"[13]

Presently, our nymph discerned through the swirling colours a citadel whose great spires towered beyond the range of sight. Its brilliance was like that of a very precious jewel, and clear as crystal.[14]

Chapter Eight

Before them stood a great open gate, made of pearl, hinged to walls of crystal. And so thick were those walls that our tree fancied not even the tallest of his forest brethren, laid lengthwise, would reach from the outside to the inside. And before that gate stood two great angels.

Led by Gabriel, the multitude streamed through, and the gate somehow seemed to widen for them. Now they could see, coming from the centre of that city, a golden light that illuminated even the brightest angel's countenance.

And to the left and right of our great multitude came two other great multitudes, who had come in through two other gates, each led by another great angel. And so it was that three great companies converged.

But what our tree beheld next was even more spectacular—a great and sparkling creature with four faces and four wings, and tall as a mountain. In awe, he trembled at its majesty. Then he realized its wings touched those of two other immense creatures on either side, and those beings touched a fourth, facing in the opposite direction. Together, they formed a vast circle.[15]

And each of the four-faced beings was

approached by three multitudes, so that there were twelve multitudes in all, each led by an angel, who entered through twelve city gates.

But now, outshining all, in the midst of the four great creatures, was a region that pulsed with lightning, and surrounded by rainbow light. And from it arose a vast and icy expanse, and upon that expanse was a great throne, the colour of sapphire, and on that throne a figure like that of a man. From the waist up, he looked like glowing metal, and from the waist down he looked like fire. And it was He whose glory illuminated that great city.[16]

Then was a great voice heard, like the sound of rushing waters: "Now is come salvation, power, and the Kingdom of God."[17]

At this, each of the twelve angels raised a trumpet to his lips and gave it breath, seizing the air with such force that the very walls of the city shook. And the great assembly cheered, and their cries shook the city to its foundations.

"The time has come!" said the great voice. "I am that star that appeared to you in the heavens. And I am come to bless thee. I established thee in Eden, thou died'st with me at Calvary, and thou art chosen to celebrate the day of my birth. Thou wilt ever stand with me by the River of Life, and thou shalt bear twelve crops of fruit, and thou shalt heal the nations."

Our tree remembered these were the very words spoken to him on the eve of Christmas, when the miniature figures on the piano had come to life and the baby creature had suddenly become a full-grown man.

And as he recalled that wondrous vision, behold, the same man appeared! Immediately, the whole multitude of nymphs and angels and divine beings, even the four-winged creatures with four faces, bowed before this man. Our tree did the same, though not out of imitation. Divine instinct seemed to guide him.

So imagine how our tree must have felt to see that man, in appearance like a servant, walk towards him. In his hands, he carried a simple wooden bowl, with water that sparkled in the reflection of divine light.

He stooped to place the bowl at the feet of our nymph,[18] who trembled to be the centre of Heaven's attention. The man took off his outer clothing, and our tree saw a red gash in his side, like the cut in the bark of a tree. Then, kneeling, the man took one of our nymph's feet and started to wash it with water from the bowl.

Now we do not know what colour a nymph turns when he blushes. Green, perhaps, or red, like us. But our nymph was certainly blushing now.

"Surely not I, Lord," he whispered. "This is an honour that I do not deserve."[19] And again, it seemed Divine Instinct was at work, that our nymph should call him "Lord".

"Thy worthiness comes from me," replied the man.

Our tree looked into the eyes of that Man of Compassion and saw their infinite love. And he wept for joy. And as he wept, an angel appeared before him, holding a golden vessel, in which he caught the tears of our tree.[20] And the tears turned to a vapour of pleasing aroma that rose to the great throne above.[21]

Having washed both feet of our nymph, the man dried them with his outer garment then gently picked him up and carried him on his back. At this, our tree felt his limbs stiffen, stretching out from his sides, forming together a straight beam crossing his body, which itself lengthened into another, longer beam.

A stream of images now appeared to him — the Man of Compassion is seated, and a woman kneels before him and pours precious oil on his feet, at which another man protests;[22] now a group of men are eating, and the one who had protested departs hurriedly from the others;[23] now the Man of

Compassion is stretched out on the ground, weeping, and crying tears of blood, while his companions sleep nearby; an armed rabble appears, and the one who had protested kisses the Man of Compassion, whereupon the rabble seize him. One man strikes off the ear of another, but the Man of Compassion straight restores it; a bird crows three times, and the man who had severed the ear is struck with grief;[24] a woman shrieks in her sleep; and a man in fine robes washes his hands.[25]

Now is our tree in the scene himself. The man carrying him wears a circle of thorns around his head, he is bleeding, his back glistens, and he stoops under the weight of our tree. They are surrounded by cruel human creatures, wearing headpieces that glare in the sunlight, topped with red feathers. They are like those creatures who cut him down in the forest, with rough hands and rougher hearts. They shout and jeer and hurl wet clods from their mouths onto the man and the tree. The man collapses, and then our tree is carried by another man.

Now is our tree being hammered and torn, sharp unyielding objects driven into the ends of his limbs. He screams in agony, as does the Man of Compassion impaled upon him. Another sharp object is driven in as he hears the mocking words: "King of the Jews."

Now is our tree vertical once more, erected upon a hill of death. He feels the weight of the Man of Compassion hanging from him, a body being ripped apart, blood trailing down his timbers, and a soul in anguish that cries out, "My God, my God. Why hast thou forsaken me?!"[26]

Death surges through him, and every manner of evil that can be named or not named — every murder, every betrayal, every disease, torture, and destruction ever visited on Creation. In blanketing, crushing, paralyzing, suffocating darkness, he knows not up from down, knows not whether he is dead or alive and longs for death, to be delivered from this everlasting horror on the brink of oblivion. All this happens in the twinkle of an eye, a myriad of images and experiences somehow encapsulated in a moment.

As waking from a nightmare, our tree found himself again on the back of the man who had just bathed his feet, but his branches were supple again, all was peaceful now, and Heaven was watching in awe.

Our tree was being carried beside a great river in Heaven,[27] and the river's banks glowed with silver hue. And our tree fancied it must be the same river where he had first encountered his sister in Paradise, though here it was much wider.

And as the man bore our tree beside the river, the golden willows that lined its banks swept their fronds and bowed in reverence until the Man of Compassion reached the anointed place. There, he handed our tree to the angel Gabriel while he scooped out a hole in the silvery ground with his hands. Then, taking our tree back from Gabriel's hands, he placed his trunk into that hole and restored the silvery earth around him.

A voice rang out again, "Now is come salvation, power, and the kingdom of God."

With that, the entire assembly of Heaven roared in joy and triumph. Our tree grew to great size, or perhaps the assembly had shrunk to miniature size. For now he was surrounded by a countless throng, who adorned him with every manner of decoration in every colour, like the decoration ceremony of his Christmas family, but of size immeasurable.

From bottom to top, the myriads dressed him. The host of pink beings adorned him with ribbon, the warriors placed upon him their great shields, and the angels hung from him bright lights of every hue.

Our tree looked and saw the splendour of his

adornments, and his heart was full of joy. The sound of voices rang out around him, and the bright colours whirled before him. Finally, Gabriel soared aloft holding a great silver star in his hands, to the sound of horns and trumpets and all manner of brass instrument.

And the splendour of Gabriel's wings beat before our tree, and the bright star dazzled his vision and mingled with dancing swirls of purple and orange and gold, that gathered into a great sphere of light that spread its warmth upon him.

And the trumpets mingled with the chorus of birdsong. And the majestic dawn stretched her pink rays into the garden. And the wings that fluttered before our tree were now those of the sparrow, who landed in his topmost branches.

Chapter Nine

Behold, it was morning, our tree's first morning in his new garden. And what a splendid morning it was! For the sun glistened upon the frost that enveloped every needle of every branch of our tree, and it shone in the water drops that gathered at the ends, and it gleamed on every blade of grass below. And fresh, scented breezes wafted across the little garden.

"How did you sleep?" enquired the little sparrow, with a glint in his little, darting eyes, and a flick in his little brown tail.

"I had a most wondrous dream!" replied our tree, then related all he had seen and heard in his magical vision of the night.

"But how my heart aches for that wondrous place, how I long to behold again the supreme being on the throne and the man who carried me to the riverbank. And how I yearn to see my sister again, but she told me I would come back here first."

"Of course!" said the sparrow. "If you did not, who would bring hope to the *other* trees?"

Then the little bird winked and flapped his wings, whence our tree's vision was overwhelmed by an intense white light. He fancied he glimpsed in the brightness a splendid being of great size speeding to the very edge of the sky, propelling himself with great beating wings, and beyond the range of height.

As our tree's sight adjusted to the brightness, he saw before him the little boy again, wearing the same pyjamas as when he had thwarted the great white beast.

"Good morning, Mr. Christmas Tree!" he said.

And the little chap fancied he saw the top of the tree nod toward him in acknowledgment.

"How splendid you look today!" said the boy. "All your colour seems to have come back."

Our tree looked down. And indeed he was restored to his former glory of the forest. And though he wished in vain to see those divinely wrought decorations just lavished upon him by the myriads of Heaven, yet was his heart glad to see that his needles were now full, thick, rich, and verdant—how they gleamed in the morning sun— and to feel the warm glow as sap flowed abundantly through his veins.

"No-one will ever cut you down again," said the boy.

And he was true to his word. The boy and his father watched diligently over the coming days and weeks to see how their tree progressed, watering him frequently and enriching the soil around with good nutrients, until they were assured that he was happily putting down roots in his new home.

Over the years, our tree grew tall and strong. And so did the boy. And every Christmas, he and his kin would decorate our tree outdoors with brightly coloured ornaments and playful lights.

And the seed of our tree was carried aloft, even beyond the bounds of the sea, and took root where it fell and populated new forests. And his descendants believed.

And the sparrow carried his message to the other birds. And our friend the tall beech tree told his fellows on the street, and they told other trees, who told the willow trees on the river banks, who whispered to each other on the night breezes throughout every land. And so from bird to bird and tree to tree, the fame of *our* tree spread far and wide.

Sometimes, a wounded bird would land in his branches. Perhaps it had been shot at by mean-spirited people or had escaped from a vicious cat or barely survived a deadly trap. And in the fronds of our tree, it would find healing. They told of these miracles, and others believed.

And the beech trees outside the family's home

were able to comfort the Christmas trees thrown out beneath them every year, with the news that a Paradise awaited them, where there was no more death, and where the Divine Countenance looks upon his loved ones with favour unearned.

And those who hoped found it to be so. They too would fly to that wondrous city with its gates of pearl and resplendent angels, and they too would behold the great being at the centre of it all.

Epilogue

Our tree saw the little boy grow into a big boy, and the big boy into a man. And one day that man was joined by a lovely female creature. And together they had their own little children, who each year would return to decorate the tree at Christmas time. And the boy's father became an older man, whom our tree likened in his imagination to a sturdy oak. And after he was no more, the tree and the boy grew to ripe old age.

By now, our tree was taller than the roof that stood between him and the beech tree, and they were able to speak to each other directly.

One night, our tree was woken from slumber by the call of his friend.

"Hey kid!" he called out—for he had always addressed our tree that way since they first met, and the term stuck, even though they were both veterans by now. "Look up!"

Our tree did so and beheld a bright star blazing across the sky towards them.

"Wow!" said the beech tree. "I neva saw nutt'n like dat befoher! Is dat what you saw in your vision ding all dose yee-ahs ago?"

"Oh yes!" whispered our tree in hushed reverence. "It is time!"

The bright star blazed ever closer.

"It's coming our way!" shouted the beech tree. "Incoming!" he roared.

All the trees on the street awoke and looked up in alarm at the bright apparition that came their way on bright wings. But *our* tree watched silently with calm anticipation.

On the vision came, until its wings were visible — wings of great flaming horses drawing a flaming conveyance with wheels full of eyes. And in this conveyance, which we might call a chariot, was a fiery being, clad in white and gold, whose face shone with a brilliance almost too bright to behold.

Now hovering just above the garden, the angel reached down. And our tree reached up. For now he had supple and muscular limbs once more, as in his vision when he met his sister. And he stepped aboard.

"Until we meet again," said our nymph, reaching down to touch the branch of the beech tree, "by the River of Life."

"See ya later, kid!" the beech tree whispered, trembling in amazement.

With that, the chariot sped away into the night sky to the great acclaim of the trees below, and beyond the limit of vision.

As our tree hurtled through otherworldly realms, another great chariot flew past in the opposite direction, drawn by great wingèd horses and steered by another great and luminous wingèd being. And our nymph knew instinctively that this conveyance was on course to fetch his friend the beech tree. And he rejoiced in his heart.

And then he saw, flying on a parallel course, a third great chariot. In it was the little boy of his first Christmas, who waved furiously. He was wearing a splendid crown of gold and diamonds, and looked quite the little prince.

"Hello!" he called.

"Hello!" our tree hailed back.

Now the chariots converged, and boy and nymph embraced in the air.

"I always knew you could talk," said the boy.

"And I always knew that you knew," said our nymph. "Thank you for saving me from the jaws of death."

"Oh, the garbage truck," said the boy. "There won't be any more of those here!"

And tears of joy wetted the cheeks of both as they flew. So much they had to share, so many experiences to relate. But that would wait. For now, swooping down from above, came the father of the boy, as he had first appeared to our tree, prime in manhood where youth ended.[28] But he had wings now. He was armed and muscular, clearly one of that great squadron of warriors who had flown alongside the multitude of nymphs on their way to the great city. He descended into the chariot and held his son in joyful embrace.

And at that moment, gracefully alighting alongside our nymph in *his* chariot, came his sister from the forest. And as our nymph held her, love surged through him and from him and over him, like a mighty river.

"There's someone who wants to see you!" she said, chuckling, then reached behind her and brought forth a squirrel, whom our tree recognized immediately. It was the same fellow who had clasped his branch in his final moments in the forest.

"Glad we meet in better circumstances!" said the squirrel, laughing.

Our nymph took hold of him and let him run up his arm and settle on his shoulder to enjoy the ride.

Thus, they all reached their destination in Paradise. Our tree was reunited with his sister, with his fellows from the great forest, with the squirrel, and with the Divine Presence who had borne him to the River of Life. How glorious were the things they saw and experienced, and there was no end to the wonders ahead.[29]

Perhaps you can imagine that wonderful place. For your imagination is a gift that enables you to see beauty, even when things seem ugly around you. Know that the Divine Presence awaits you too, Paradise longs to embrace *you*, and that our nymph and his friends will meet you there!

THE END

Get a FREE book when you join Abdiel's Readers List at poetprophet.com/contact, along with advance notification of upcoming giveaways.

About the Author

Thank you for purchasing *The Christmas Tree*, and if you enjoyed it, please leave a review at Amazon US or Amazon UK, as this is enormously helpful for an independent author and assists other readers to discover his books.

Abdiel is a British-American author and actor whose life is largely inspired by the Bible, Shakespeare, mythology, and the great epic poem, *Paradise Lost*. He has memorized thousands of lines of poetry and can come up with an instant quote for every occasion!

These inspirations are especially evident in his own epic poems. Abdiel's signature work, *Elijah*, reimagines the great Old-Testament prophet's ministry and miracles, while his "little epic", *Obama's Dream*, takes the former president on a night-time journey of transformation while exposing the destructive traits of empire handed over to Donald Trump!

Political theatre is also seen through the lens of poetry in *Verses Versus Empire*, Abdiel's three-volume series covering in turn the Bush, Obama, and Trump eras. His other collections include *Well Versed: To Shakespeare, Poets, and the Performing Arts*, which features poems voiced by famed British actors in BBC broadcasts, among them Kenneth Branagh, Judi Dench, and Mark Rylance.

But Abdiel's *own* skills as a narrator and voice actor make for especially dramatic readings. You can hear excerpts from all his books at poetprophet.com.

In non-fiction, Abdiel has published *Dueling the Dragon: Adventures in Chinese Media and Education*, a memoir crafted over 10 years as he lived and worked in China. And *The Gourmet Gospel: A Spiritual Path to Guilt-Free Eating* shows how the grace of God transforms us and sets the conscience free, especially when it comes to "merciful munching"!

As an actor, Abdiel has embodied most of the major Shakespearean roles, and on stages from New York to London to Beijing, though perhaps his most famous appearance is in the hit short film series, *The Expert*. He has also staged three one-man shows, including the immortal children's tale,

Wind in the Willows.

Abdiel's previous careers include broadcasting and financial analysis. His passions encompass Argentine Tango, Yoga, and competitive Swimming.

Author website: poetprophet.com/about

Books by
Abdiel LeRoy

Non-fiction

The Gourmet Gospel
A Spiritual Path to Guilt-Free Eating

Ever felt guilty about how much you eat? Or what you eat? Or when you eat? Let this book dispel your guilt!

Using principles from the Bible and great thinkers, *The Gourmet Gospel* will lead you to freedom of conscience in every aspect of life, and especially when it comes to "merciful munching".

Dueling the Dragon
Adventures in Chinese Media and Education

A wide-eyed expat is detained by Beijing cops and told to sign a false confession. Will he make it out of China alive? *Dueling the Dragon* is a great adventure story, but *this* one just happens to be true!

With a journalist's eye and lively wit, LeRoy exposes the deep levels of corruption tearing at China's social fabric.

Epic Poems

Obama's Dream
The Journey That Changed the World

This little theatre we call politics
Is full of lies and dirty tricks,
But what if angels came into the fray
To challenge presidents and what they say?

And what if one appeared before God's throne
Where wicked schemes of men are overthrown
And Satan tried a victim to condemn?
This book turns upside-down the world of men!

Elijah
A Prophet's Tale

He called down fire and false prophets slew,
He raised the dead, conversed with angels, flew
To Heaven in a chariot of fire
And fled from Jezebel's murderous ire.

But there is more, O so much more to tell:
Of meeting Moses and a dragon's spell,
Shapeshifting goddesses at Cherith Brook.
Such wonders will unfold within this book!

Poetry Collections

Verses Versus Empire: III — The Trump Era

The intellectuals of this dangerous age,
However eloquent, however sage,
Indicting empire with insightful prose,
Have not yet healed America's woes.

To tear down strongholds of the powers-that-be
Who give lip service to Democracy,
A poet of prophetic voice steps forward
To prove the pen is mightier than the sword!

Verses Versus Empire: II — The Obama Era

As the late historian Howard Zinn said, "There have only been a handful of people who use their wit to take down the pretensions of the high and mighty."

Here is one of them, a resounding voice for our times, an offering of hope and beauty rising from the ashes of our broken political system, a creation of unprecedented literary power. Witness herein that the pen really *is* mightier than the sword!

Verses Versus Empire: I — The Bush Era

It's Judgment Day, and George W. Bush strides confidently towards the throne of God. How will the Almighty respond? Find out in this work of devastating satire!

From Bush through Obama to Trump, LeRoy charts an epic course through the inferno of U.S. politics, exposing the fraud and folly of empire and its rulers.

Well Versed
To Shakespeare, Poets, and the Performing Arts

Dante is famous. He imagined Hell,
A plain of burning flakes and sulphurous smell,
Pour souls afflicted in a sorry state,
And names the enemies he loves to hate.

But he's no match for Milton's inspiration,
No poet greater in imagination.
Yet Shakespeare most gets ink within these pages.
'Twas he who said, "Our praises are our wages!"

Fiction

The Christmas Tree

From the heart of an ancient forest, whispered love awakens the courage of a little boy to protect his beloved tree. But can he overcome man's impulse to destroy, his merciless machinery, his callous indifference?

This magical tale will impart a hope that embraces all of humanity, a testament to love in this world and the next, introducing young readers to themes of resurrection and care for the environment.

Notes

1   Luke 1:42.

2   Revelation 1:15.

3   From Shakespeare's *The Merchant of Venice*, V.i.

4   Matthew 2:9.

5   Luke 2:8-20.

6   Ezekiel 47:12; Revelation 22:2.

7   Borrowing a phrase from Kenneth Grahame's *Wind in the Willows*: "Mole and Rat kicked the fire up, drew their chairs in, brewed themselves a last nightcap of mulled ale, and discussed the events of the long day."

8   Echoing Oscar Wilde in *The Picture of Dorian Gray*: "...that strange interest in trivial things that we try to develop when things of high import make us afraid..."

9   Revelation 21:4.

10   Matthew 3:17, 17:5; Mark 1:11; Luke 3:22; 2 Peter 1:17.

11   A phrase taken from W.H. Auden's poem, *As I Walked Out One Evening*.

12   Isaiah 6:6-7.

13   Luke 1:19.

14   Revelation 21:10-21.

15   Ezekiel 1:4-24.

16   Ezekiel 1:25-28.

17   Revelation 12:10.

18   Psalm 18:35.

19   John 13:8.

20   Psalm 56:8.

21   Revelation 5:8.

22   John 12:1-6.

23   John 13:30.

24   Luke 22:44-62.

25   Matthew 27:19-24.

26   Matthew 27:27-50.

27 Revelation 22:1-2.

28 A phrase taken from John Milton's *Paradise Lost*, Book XI, where he describes the archangel Michael's human guise.

29 Isaiah 9:7.

25478877R00057

Made in the USA
Middletown, DE
18 December 2018